Karna
The Greatest Archer in the World

Vatsala Sperling

Illustrated by Sandeep Johari

Bear Cub Books
Rochester, Vermont

For Dada, Harish Johari, and for
adoptive parents and children everywhere

Special thanks to Eliza Thomas for her editorial support

Bear Cub Books
One Park Street
Rochester, Vermont 05767
www.InnerTraditions.com

Bear Cub Books is a division of Inner Traditions International

Text copyright © 2007 by Vatsala Sperling
Artwork copyright © 2007 by Sandeep Johari

Library of Congress Cataloging-in-Publication Data

Sperling, Vatsala, 1961–

    Karna : the greatest archer in the world / Vatsala Sperling ; illustrated by Sandeep Johari.

      p. cm.

    ISBN-13: 978-1-59143-073-5 (hardcover)

    ISBN-10: 1-59143-073-9 (hardcover)

    1. Karna (Hindu mythology)—Juvenile literature. 2. Karna (Hindu mythology)—Pictorial works—Juvenile literature. I. Johari, Sandeep, ill. II. Title.

    BL1138.4.K37S74 2007

    294.5'92304521—dc22

                                            2007018799

Printed and bound in India by Replika Press Pvt. Ltd.

10 9 8 7 6 5 4 3 2 1

Text design and layout by Virginia Scott Bowman
This book was typeset in Berkeley with Abbess and Nueva as display typefaces

To send correspondence to the author of this book, mail a first-class letter to the author c/o Inner Traditions • Bear & Company, One Park Street, Rochester, VT 05767, and we will forward the communication.

A Cast of Characters

Kunti (Kun-'tee)
A royal princess, birth mother of Karna; later wife of King Pandu and mother of the first three Pandava brothers

Durvasa
(Dur-'vaah-'saah)
The sage who gives Kunti a secret mantra for calling the gods

The Sun God
Birth father of Karna

Adhiratha
(Ad-hi-raht-'haah)
Karna's adoptive father, husband of Radha

Radha
(Rah-'dhaah)
Karna's adoptive mother, wife of Adhiratha

Karna
(Kar-'naah)
Son born to Princess Kunti and the Sun God, adopted by Adhiratha and Radha

Pandu
('Paahn-doo)
King of Hastinapur, husband of Kunti and Madri, father of the Pandava brothers

Dhritrashtra
(Dhrit-'raah-strah)
King Pandu's blind brother, father of Duryodhana

Gandhari
('Gaahn-'dhaa-ree)
Wife of Dhritrashtra, mother of Duryodhana. She wears a blindfold to empathize with her blind husband.

Duryodhana
(Dur-'yoh-dhan)
Firstborn son of Dhritrashtra and Gandhari; greedy cousin of the Pandava brothers

The Pandava ('Paahn-da-va) **brothers Yudhishthira** (Yudh-'eesh-tira), **Bhima** ('Bhee-ma), and **Arjuna** (Ar-'joo-na), are sons of Kunti and Pandu. **Nakula** ('Nah-koo-la) and **Sahadeva** (Sa-'ha-day-vah) are sons of Pandu and Madri. All of the Pandava brothers are half human, half god.

Sage Parasuram
(Parah-shu-'raahm)
The sage who teaches archery to Karna

Shakuni
(Sha-ku-'nee)
Duryodhana's crafty uncle, Gandhari's brother

Krishna
('Krish-na)
Vishnu, God of Preservation, born on Earth as a nephew of Kunti

Indra
('In-dra)
God of Thunder and Lightning, disguised as a Brahmin

About Karna

The Mahabharata is an ancient epic from India that tells of a war between two branches of a royal family. The five Pandava princes fight for justice, goodness, and fairness, while their greedy cousin Duryodhana and his ninety-nine siblings represent the darker side of human nature. Half human and half god, Karna is a member of this warring family, but he doesn't know this because he was abandoned at birth.

Adopted by a poor couple, Adhiratha and Radha, Karna is raised with love. Although his adoptive parents know nothing about weapons and warfare, they give Karna the courage to follow his heart's desire—to become the greatest archer in the world. In return, he honors them above all others. In their loving home, Karna learns to trust his own generous heart when faced with life's difficult decisions. His heart tells him that promises are meant for keeping and life is meant for giving. Although he always tries to do the right thing, like all of us, Karna makes mistakes. In the end, his mistakes cost him his very life, but they never cost him his honor. To this day he is remembered in India as the greatest archer in the world and as the most generous person ever born.

A long time ago, a beautiful young princess named Kunti lived with her uncle, King Kuntibhoj, in a lovely palace along the banks of a wide river. One day, when she was twelve years old, her uncle said to her, "Kunti, an important visitor will be arriving soon. Sage Durvasa is very learned and we are honored to receive him as our royal guest, but he's well known for his terrible temper. Child, I'm asking you to make sure all his needs are taken care of. Give him no reason at all to become angry. Please do be careful, Kunti, the future of my kingdom depends on you. Sage Durvasa has the power to put terrible curses on anyone who displeases him!"

"Yes, Uncle," Kunti promised, and soon she turned herself into a most perfect hostess. She could almost read Sage Durvasa's mind and met his every need before he realized anything was wanting. The sage had a very peaceful and happy stay and wanted to reward Kunti for her services. He studied her face and used his magic powers to see into her future. "Child," he said, "one day you will need the help of the gods. I am going to teach you a secret mantra for inviting the gods into your life. Be very careful with this mantra! Use it wisely." Kunti repeated the syllables after him. She promised to use the mantra only in times of great need.

But Kunti was only twelve, after all, and she was a lively and curious girl. Early the next morning she was playing by herself in the royal garden. The sun had risen and Kunti watched as its rays touched a flower here, a leaf there. She felt its warmth on her skin. She thought about the Sun God waking up the whole world. *I wonder . . .* she thought. *I wonder if the Sun would come to me.* Forgetting her promise to Durvasa, she began to recite the mantra. She closed her eyes and concentrated the way she had been taught. Soon her body became prickly hot, as if she were sitting by a fire. She could hear the fire roar and crackle! She opened her eyes to see a glowing chariot swooping down from the heavens. It was pulled by seven horses—and the Sun God himself was driving them! "You called me," Sun said, stepping from the carriage with a baby in his arms. "You called me," he said again, placing the baby in her lap, "and I bring you my son."

Kunti looked at the baby. *Oh no!* she thought. *What have I done?* "Sun," she wailed. "I am only twelve years old! I didn't know what I was doing. Please! Take your baby away!" Her cries mingled with the cries of the infant in her lap. "Please! I am not ready to be a mother!"

"You used the sacred mantra," the Sun God replied. "The baby is your responsibility now. But I leave him with divine gifts. Look—he has a pair of golden earrings and wears a golden shield on his chest. They will grow with him. As long as he wears them, he cannot be killed." The Sun God sped off into the morning sky, leaving poor Kunti alone with a newborn babe in her arms.

She was panic-stricken. What a string of curses Sage Durvasa would hurl at her now! She would live in shame! Who would ever believe that the Sun God had brought her a child? Then she looked again at the baby, squirming in her arms, shimmering with celestial light just like his father. She rocked him gently. His cries quieted, and Kunti realized that she had stopped crying, too. "Alas, I cannot be your mother," she said sadly. "I am much too young. I will have to let you go."

Kunti found a sturdy basket, some wax, and cloth of the softest silk. She coated the basket with the wax to make it waterproof, and lined it with layers of the silk to make it soft and warm. She placed the baby carefully in his new bed and carried the basket to the river. Then she kissed him good-bye and set the basket afloat. "Farewell," she whispered. "May the Sun God watch over you always and keep you safe. May you find parents who will love you and care for you. I will always remember you." Drying her tears as best she could, she walked slowly back to the palace.

The tiny basket bounced up and down in the current, but Kunti had made it well, and the baby never even got wet. Sun hovered above and cloaked himself in a veil of clouds so as not to melt the wax of the basket—though every now and again he sent down a ray or two, to keep the baby nice and warm.

Downstream, Adhiratha was sitting on a rock, hoping to catch a fish for the midday meal. He was a gentle and good man, a charioteer by trade, and his wife Radha was a gentle and good woman. They were often sad, however, for they were unable to have children. How they longed for a baby of their own! Adhiratha sighed as he thought about their lonely life. He cast the line out over the river and sighed again. But what was that at the bend in the river, illuminated by a single ray peeking through the clouds? Adhiratha waded out into the current and caught hold of the basket. When he saw its precious cargo he was at a complete loss for words. "Oh!" he gasped as he ran all the way home, carrying the basket in his arms. "Oh!" he gasped as he stood dripping in the doorway, holding the basket out for his dear wife to see. When Radha saw the tiny baby lying peacefully asleep, his earrings and shield glowing like golden flames, she was speechless, too. "Oh! Oh! Oh!" she gasped. When the baby woke up and gave a little cry, Radha's breast filled with milk as if by magic. She picked the baby up and let him nurse to his heart's content. Finally, she found just the right words. "Our son is beautiful!" she said.

Born to a princess and the Sun, this baby was half royal and half divine, and he was indeed a beautiful child. Adhiratha and Radha did not know his origin but they adored him just the same. The couple named their new son Vasushena, which means "born with shield and earrings," and they raised him as their own. Adhiratha and Radha considered themselves blessed, and the three made a very happy family. Their small cottage was richer than the largest palace of the kingdom, for within its humble walls this cottage held love. Later Vasushena came to be known as Karna, and so we shall call him Karna as his story continues.

Years passed. As Karna grew to be a sweet and energetic little boy, Kunti became a graceful young woman and married King Pandu of Hastinapur. In days of old, Indian kings could marry more than one wife. Along with Kunti, King Pandu married another princess named Madri. Before the newlyweds could settle down together, however, King Pandu set off to fight a war against the neighboring kingdoms, leaving his blind brother Dhritrashtra to rule in his place. Dhritrashtra secretly hoped Pandu would stay away forever. He wanted one of his own sons to inherit the throne.

Soon after returning from war, King Pandu left again on a honeymoon with his wives. They were happy to be together, but alas, their bliss was soon destroyed. While out hunting one morning, King Pandu took aim at a pair of deer, killing the doe. Unbeknownst to the king, the two deer were actually a sage and his wife in disguise. Horrified, the king watched as the doe changed into the body of a dead woman, while her mate transformed into the figure of a sage. "I am so sorry! I am so terribly sorry!" Pandu kept saying. But the sage was distraught with grief, and cursed Pandu. "I will never again feel my wife's tender embrace," he said. "As punishment, the moment you embrace your wives, you, too, will die!"

Pandu told Kunti and Madri the terrible news. "I love you, but I can never touch you," he said. "We will never have children together!" Kunti was quiet for a while. She thought to herself, *This time, I am ready to care for a baby.* She told Pandu about the mantra for inviting the gods—although she didn't tell him she had used it once before—and he readily agreed to let her try it. Kunti used the mantra to summon Dharmaraj, the lord of justice, and soon she gave birth to a beautiful baby boy. The new parents were ecstatic and they named their son Yudhishthira. Over the following years two more sons arrived: Bhima, son of Pavan, the wind god, and Arjuna, son of Indra, the god of thunder and lightning. When Kunti taught the mantra to Madri, she was blessed with twin sons, Nakul and Sahadev, whose father was Ashwini, the god of youth and beauty. These five princes came to be known as the Pandava brothers. As was the custom, all of them called both Kunti and Madri "Mother."

Meanwhile, Dhritrashtra's wife Gandhari also became pregnant. The pregnancy, however, lasted for two long years, and when she gave birth, it was not to a baby, but rather to a strange round object, hard as iron and hot as burning coal. She lamented bitterly, sure that she would never again bear a son or daughter. Dhritrashtra's grandfather, Sage Vyasa, heard Gandhari weeping and came to console her.

"I can help," he said. "Don't worry." In a secret chamber, he filled one hundred and one earthen pots with a magic potion. Then he broke the strange object into little pieces, and dropped them one by one into the pots. He instructed that no one should disturb the pots or lift up the lids or even step in to the secret chamber.

Two years later, hearing a huge commotion, Queen Gandhari and Grandfather Bhishma, a wise old man of the court of Hastinapur, rushed into the secret room. The pots were rolling and crashing about, and the air was filled with sounds of whimpering and cooing. Because of her blindfold, Gandhari couldn't see the source of all the uproar. But imagine her joy when Grandfather Bhishma told her that the room held one hundred newborn boys and one baby girl with drops of the magic potion still glistening on their soft skin!

Then one of the babies started to scream, his face twisted with rage. Red sparks flew from his eyes and ears and mouth. Black crows circled above his pot, and wolves skulked nearby. Grandfather Bhishma knew that the wolves and crows were bad omens. He warned Gandhari and Dhritrashtra, saying, "You must send this one away to Grandfather Vyasa. He will know how to raise him well."

But the king and queen ignored this advice. The baby seemed so strong! Surely he would be the one to inherit the throne. They named him Duryodhana and lavished him with attention.

As Bhishma feared, Duryodhana proved to be a very nasty little boy. He wrapped his parents around his little finger, while they spoiled him shamelessly. When he got his own way he seemed nice enough, but woe to anyone who crossed him! All the maids and servants and his ninety-nine brothers and one sister lived in fear of his cruel tricks.

In contrast, the five Pandava brothers lived together in harmony. The younger boys always minded Yudhishthira, their oldest brother, and they all were devoted to their parents. They studied the sacred texts together and learned the basic skills of hunting and self-defense. They were respectful of and obedient to their parents and their tutors.

In a few years, however, both Pandu and Madri died. Kunti and the children had to leave their forest home and went to live in Hastinapur. Dhritrashtra hated having his nephews in court, especially Yudhishthira, who as eldest stood to inherit the throne. Prince Duryodhana, of course, detested his five cousins. Queen Gandhari's cunning brother, Uncle Shakuni, fanned the flames of hatred and jealousy. Fights broke out constantly. It was certainly a good thing that the Pandava brothers were well trained in the arts of self-defense!

The Sages Kripa and Drona were in charge of educating both the Pandava brothers and all the children of King Dhritrashtra. They soon noticed that the Pandava brothers were gifted with divine abilities. Arjuna, in particular, excelled as an archer, and Sage Drona trained him carefully in the art of weaponry.

In the meantime, Karna, in the humble home of his adoptive parents, showed great abilities, too. He grew tall and strong, and glowed with inner beauty. Among his many excellent qualities, perhaps the most outstanding was his great generosity. At his daily midday worship of the sun, he focused his prayers on the act of giving; he was known far and wide as one of those rare people who would give the shirt off his own back, without hesitation and without a second thought.

Radha and Adhiratha adored their handsome, generous son. Radha showered him with affection. When he ran into the house after playing with his bow and arrows in the yard, she would scoop him up in her arms, mud and all, saying "I love you, I love you, I *love* you!" and Karna would bury his face in her lap happily and say, "I love you, too, Mother!"

Adhiratha was a kind and patient father who hoped to teach his son the art of training horses. But Karna had no interest in this trade. "Please, Father," he would say. "I want to be an archer." The little boy would hold up his beloved bow and arrows and smile his winning smile. "I want to be the very greatest archer in the whole wide world!"

As it turned out, this was more than a mere boyhood fantasy. Karna had a recurring dream that reflected his future as well as his past. In this dream he would see a basket floating in a river. Downstream, the water turned to blood. Bodies lay scattered about. Karna would try to run but would find himself unable to move. When he awoke he would be drenched in sweat, his heart pounding. One day he told his mother about the dream. She was silent for a moment. Then she drew him close.

"Dearest son," she began. "You are old enough to know how you came to us." She told him the whole story. She explained how much they had yearned for children, how Adhiratha had found him in the basket, and how all they could say at first was "Oh! Oh! Oh!" because they couldn't find the words to express their joy. She said, "You were wrapped in soft silk, and wore the gold earrings and shield that you still wear. We thought maybe your mother was a princess who, for some reason, could not raise you and had to let you go. May the gods bless her, she gave us a son."

Radha kissed Karna and put her arms around him. She continued, "That is what the basket means. But I'm not sure what the rest of your dream is about. Perhaps it shows that war is filled with bloodshed and violence. You seem to be drawn to the life of a warrior, but we hope you will choose the path of peace and learn your father's trade instead. We will not hold you back, though. You must follow your heart. You know we will love you always, whatever you decide." Karna hugged her tight. "Thank you," he said.

His parents' love indeed gave Karna the courage to follow his heart, and when he was old enough, he left home to seek out Sage Parasuram, who was known far and wide as the very best archery teacher. Karna knew that Sage Parasuram's school accepted only students of the Brahmin caste, but so strong was his ambition to excel at archery that he chose to masquerade as a Brahmin lad in order to gain admittance. Karna had no way of knowing who his birth parents were but he did know that his adoptive father was a tradesman, certainly not a Brahmin. Nevertheless, he presented himself to Sage Parasuram in a white dhoti and shawl, taking care to cover his golden shield. He had shaved his head, leaving nothing but a thin tuft of hair at the very top, and looked just like a young Brahmin boy ready to start training for the priesthood, the profession most Brahmins practiced.

Sage Parasuram never suspected that such a fine boy would lie about his background, and readily took him on as his student. Karna spent many years learning everything his teacher had to offer. One afternoon as the old sage was taking a nap, resting his head on Karna's lap, a ghastly bug with enormous pincers landed on Karna's thigh. It tore a deep wound in the boy's flesh, and blood gushed down his leg.

Karna sat quietly through this ordeal. Generous as always, his first thought was for his teacher. He didn't want to disturb his nap. But Sage Parasuram awoke anyway, and saw the ragged, gaping wound. *Who could withstand such pain?* the sage thought suddenly. *Only a born warrior, someone of the Kshatriya caste!*

He sat up abruptly. "Tell the truth, Karna. Who are you?"

Karna knew it was useless to pretend any longer. He told the teacher all he knew about his past.

The sage was angry and hurt. "I have loved you and trusted you," he said. "You are the finest archer I have ever taught. But for years you have chosen to deceive me." Karna bowed his head as the sage continued. "As a consequence of your lies, when you most need them, you will forget the lessons you have learned through your deceit." Turning away sadly, Sage Parasuram dismissed his beloved student. "Go now. Leave this place forever."

Heartbroken, Karna roamed the countryside. He felt completely lost. He continued with his daily practice of archery, but carelessly and without taking proper aim. One day, his arrow struck a little calf in a nearby field. The calf belonged to a poor Brahmin, who stumbled through the woods to find Karna sitting on a rock, completely unaware of what had happened.

"You have killed my calf!" the Brahmin cried in anguish. "My sacred calf, my only source of livelihood! You have left me trapped in poverty!" The poor Brahmin shook his fist at Karna as he cursed him. "May a time come when you are trapped as well. May you find yourself unable to budge—unable to lift a finger to save your own life!"

Karna offered to pay for the calf; he offered to buy the man another; he offered to work to make up for the loss. Again and again he said how sorry he was. But nothing comforted the Brahmin's grief or calmed his rage. "Get out of my sight, you cursed man!" he shouted.

I am indeed a cursed man! Karna thought. *First I earn the wrath of my teacher, and now this poor Brahmin!* Deeply unhappy, he wandered the land like a leaf caught in the wind, with no idea where to turn or what to do next.

One day months later, Karna heard news of an archery tournament, and, for the first time since his teacher dismissed him, he felt a glimmer of hope. The princes of Hastinapur were planning to display their skills to their citizens. Sage Drona had vowed that Arjuna would be named the best archer in the world. *There can't be two best archers. It is either him or me!* thought Karna, and with renewed determination he headed off to challenge Arjuna.

In Hastinapur, lavish preparations had been made. There was a huge stadium for the thousands of spectators, and vast arenas for the competitors. The citizens vied with each other for the best seats. The royal family was seated under a bright and colorful tent.

One by one the princes showed off their skills. There were sword fights, wrestling, chariot races, horse races, and elephant battles. Karna sat patiently. Finally Arjuna was announced: "The greatest archer in the world!" Arjuna showed absolute command. Not one arrow missed its mark. Not once did he hesitate or retake a shot. He was perfect. Amid the applause, Karna stood up, his figure tall and proud, his gold earrings and shield gleaming in the sun as he walked into the arena. Every face turned to stare at this unknown challenger. A hush fell over the crowd. "There can be only one greatest archer in the world," Karna shouted. "Let it be decided now." His first arrow brought down a torrent of rain. With the second arrow, the rain ceased. He shot an arrow that burst into flames, then aimed another to extinguish them. He drew his bow and then vanished, only to reappear at the other end of the stadium. The stunned public broke into thunderous cheers.

Karna aimed his next arrow straight at Arjuna. "You must fight me, Arjuna, or accept that *I* am the greatest archer in the world."

The sun shone brightly, and Karna's golden ornaments were visible for miles. Kunti was watching from the royal tent, and when she saw the glint of reflected light, she realized who the challenger must be. Her heart brimmed with joy and relief to see Karna alive and well. But she was terrified to see her two sons preparing to do battle with each other. The powerful mix of emotions overwhelmed her. She fainted and was carried back to the palace.

In the meantime, Sage Kripa intervened. "Princes of Hastinapur only accept challenges from other princes. What kingdom and what ruling family do you represent?"

Karna stood silently. What could he say? His father was a charioteer. He had no way of knowing whether or not he had royal blood. The crowd began to jeer. "A commoner, a commoner!"

Then Duryodhana, the manipulative and greedy son of Gandhari and Dhritrashtra, had an idea. Perhaps he could use Karna's skill and valor to defeat the Pandava brothers! Then he could inherit the throne! Duryodhana stood up and announced, "Here and now, I offer this fine archer the kingdom of Anga. As its king, he can compete against Arjuna." An amazed crowd fell silent again. What a turn of events! Karna had won—and then he had been disqualified—and now he was being made a king! What would happen next?

"How can I ever repay you?" Karna asked Duryodhana after receiving his crown.

"With everlasting friendship and loyalty," said Duryodhana.

"They are yours," said Karna without hesitation.

Adhiratha was also among the spectators. He, too, had recognized Karna from afar and rushed over to see what was happening. Karna rose from his new throne and ran to embrace him, saying, "Dear Father, I seek your blessings." Tears of pride and happiness streamed down Adhiratha's face.

However, it was decided that since Karna was not of royal blood (at least not as far as anyone knew) Arjuna could not accept his challenge. At the end of the day, the princes returned to their palaces and the citizens returned to their homes. Nevertheless, much had changed for everyone, and the balance of power in the world had shifted to the forces of the wicked Duryodhana.

Within the next few years, all the princes had married. It was decided that a barren stretch of land near a river would be given to the five Pandava princes, while Duryodhana would continue to be the crown prince and ruler of Hastinapur. The Pandava brothers, working together, managed to turn the wasteland into a paradise, which they named Indraprastha. Yudhishthira, the eldest, ruled with justice and compassion. The citizens prospered and were content.

Even though Duryodhana ruled over Hastinapur, he was not satisfied. The greedy fellow always wanted more, and he couldn't bear to see anyone else prospering. His wily uncle Shakuni had a suggestion. "Invite Yudhishthira for a game of dice. I'm an expert," he said with a snicker.

Uncle Shakuni was indeed an expert—at cheating. He knew how to trick his opponent into betting more and more and more and poor Yudhishthira allowed himself to be led into every trap that Uncle Shakuni laid for him. Yudhishthira bet his kingdom, his wealth, his brothers' wealth, even his own wife—and lost it all. Shakuni cheated him out of everything.

The evening resulted in total humiliation for the Pandava brothers, for Duryodhana demanded that the losers go into exile for thirteen years. Dhritrashtra was delighted. He thought, *With the Pandava brothers gone, surely my son will inherit the throne!* He was also pleased to see that Karna remained loyal to Duryodhana. *With Karna on our side, we will destroy the brothers once and for all*, he thought.

At the end of the thirteen years, the Pandava brothers returned to Hastinapur. But Duryodhana refused to give them back their land.

Lord Krishna, a god who had come to Earth from the heavens, knew how the Pandava brothers had been cheated out of their land, and he decided to step in. Born on Earth as Queen Kunti's nephew, he was allowed to address the royal court, where he tried to convince Duryodhana to relent. But even when the god himself intervened, Duryodhana refused.

"Never!" he said. "I will not give them land equal to the tip of a needle!"

"I came as an ambassador of peace," said Krishna. "But I see that war will be the only way to bring justice." He glared at the courtiers. "You are allowing cheaters and tricksters to rule the land. The Pandava brothers will avenge the injustice done to them."

At these words, Earth gave a sigh of relief. She knew that Lord Krishna would help to restore the balance of power and rid the world of evil.

Sun, however, saw bad omens and feared for his son Karna's life. He called to Karna in a dream. "Karna, beware. Lord Indra will visit you. He will be dressed like a Brahmin. He will ask for the golden earrings and shield I gave to you as a baby. Your mother knows that these charms keep you safe. If you give them away, you will die. My son, beware. Do not give them away." As Karna stirred, the dream ended. The fragments that he could remember in the morning puzzled him. He thought, *Why would Sun call me "my son"? Who was the woman that Sun called "your mother"?*

The next day at noon, during his midday worship, Karna noticed something strange. The sun shone bright in a cloudless sky, but he heard thunder in the distance. *Ah,* he thought. *Sun and Indra are trying to outdo each other!* Something stirred in his memory—was this part of his dream? Then he heard another rumble of thunder and looked around. A Brahmin was approaching.

"Please," said the man, "would you give me your earrings and your shield?"

"Of course," said Karna, generous as always. "They are yours." Heedless of the warning he had received in his dream the night before, with his knife he cut off the earrings and cut away the golden shield, leaving raw wounds in their place.

"I admire your courage and generosity," said Lord Indra—for it was indeed he. As he ran his fingers over Karna's wounds, the skin healed without a trace of scarring, flawless and shimmering as before. "Accept this gift in return," Lord Indra continued. "You may use it once. If you miss your target, the weapon will come back to me. Aim well, and your enemy will surely die." With these words, he held out a long, gleaming spear.

"Thank you, my Lord," Karna said, and bowed his head in greeting and recognition. When he looked up again, the Brahmin was gone.

Karna soon received another visit from the gods. Lord Krishna had discovered Kunti's secret long before, and knew that Karna was her son. After his efforts toward peace at Hastinapur failed, he approached Karna. "No one can escape battle, but you can choose your side. Side with the Pandava brothers, who are good men. Leave Duryodhana, who is a greedy despot. Fight on the side of justice."

"I will not leave my friend at his time of greatest need," Karna answered. "When everyone at the stadium jeered me he offered support and embraced me warmly. The Pandavas insult me and sneer at my birth. Duryodhana respects me for my skills. For all his evil acts, he is my friend." Karna's voice grew passionate. "I will not deceive a friend— neither from fear, nor temptation, nor coaxing. I would rather die." Lord Krishna heard the resolve in Karna's voice, and knew it would be pointless to push him any further.

Queen Kunti, too, attempted to convince Karna to leave Duryodhana. She knew that Duryodhana would use Karna in an effort to destroy her five sons. She also knew that without Karna, Duryodhana would not have the courage to go to war. And she couldn't bear the thought of her sons battling one another. *It is time to tell Karna the truth about his birth. Surely the truth will sway him*, she thought. She approached Karna just as he was completing his midday meditation.

"What can I do for you, Queen Kunti?" Karna asked.

Kunti took a deep breath and began. "You must call me 'Mother,'" she said. "I was twelve years old when you were born to me, and I hadn't seen you again until the archery contest. But I recognized you in the stadium. Even as a newborn babe you wore the golden earrings and shield that Sun, your father, had given you." Her voice began to shake, but she steadied herself. "Dear son, you must try to understand. I was so young when you were born to me! I was so afraid! I had to send you away, but I tried my best to send you safely." She reached out and put her hand on Karna's shoulder. "My son, please join the Pandava princes. You must not fight your brothers. They will welcome you as their older brother. Duryodhana is a bad man. I don't want any of my sons to die. . . ." Kunti's voice trailed into a soft sob.

Thus Karna finally learned who his birth parents were. For years and years he had wondered. He thought, *How strange, now that I know, the truth makes little difference.* "Thank you, Queen Kunti," he said formally.

Kunti said again, "Please, call me 'Mother.'"

"No," said Karna. "I cannot. You, too, must try to understand. When I was hungry and needed mother's milk, it was not you who fed me. When I got hurt, it was not you who kissed my cuts and bruises. When I had nightmares, it was not you who comforted me. When I was mocked and jeered at the stadium, it was not you who claimed me. It was not you who ran to embrace me."

"But I couldn't. I had fainted." Kunti tried to explain, tried to excuse herself, but Karna cut her off.

"You say that you are my mother. No. My mother is Radha, and for all her poverty, she outshines any royalty or riches. You tell me that Sun is my father. But the sun pales in greatness next to my father, the humble Adhiratha. They are the parents who took me in when I was homeless and abandoned, who raised me and cared for me." Now his voice, too, was shaking. "They are the ones who loved me. You, Queen Kunti, are the one who cast me away."

Karna and Kunti were both sobbing now. For an instant they embraced as mother and son—then just as quickly they released each other. There was a chasm between them that only time might bridge. But time was the one thing they did not have.

"Queen Kunti, how can you, of all people, ask me to abandon a friend?" said Karna. "But I cannot refuse anyone," he continued with a bitter smile. "I will honor your request. You want your sons to survive. My enmity is only with Arjuna. If I kill him, or if he kills me, you will still have five sons as before. I promise not to kill your other four sons."

Kunti left with a sad heart. It was too late to prevent this terrible war. Karna's heart was heavy also. For him, too, the war loomed darkly. He could not bring himself to abandon a friend, as he himself had once been abandoned. He knew, though, that the coming battle would pitch good against evil. Through loyalty to Duryodhana, he was pledged to the wrong side. Deep in his heart, Karna understood that he himself must die so that good might prevail. He would fight hard, but he would lose. He walked slowly away. He knew each step took him closer to his own death.

The war was fierce and intense. Lord Krishna joined as Arjuna's charioteer and protector, and the chariot flew from one end of the battlefield to the other. Lord Krishna was especially vigilant when Karna drew near. After eighteen days of battling, he saw Karna draw out the spear Lord Indra had given him, aiming to hurl it directly at Arjuna's head. Karna was an exceptional warrior who never missed his mark, and Indra's spear was deadly. So Krishna shifted his weight abruptly, tipping the chariot at a sharp angle. Arjuna, startled, lost his balance and fell—and the spear just missed its mark. It bounced off Arjuna's crown and returned to Lord Indra in a bolt of lightning.

Karna continued to fight fearlessly for his friend Duryodhana. But in the end, his old mistakes returned to haunt him, and the old curses were fulfilled. In the final moments, the back wheel of Karna's chariot sank in deep mud. He tried to pry the wheel loose, but it refused to budge. Karna was trapped, just as the old Brahmin had foretold. He tried to send an arrow toward Arjuna, but suddenly he couldn't remember how to use his bow, just as Parasuram had predicted. Lord Krishna signaled quickly to Arjuna, "Now! It is your only opportunity!" Arjuna took aim and Karna didn't have a chance. He had given away the earrings and shield, the sacred gifts that would have protected him.

Karna's last thoughts were for Radha and Adhiratha, his beloved parents. As he lay dying, he sent them all his love. The generous Karna, though he had made fatal choices, had truly lived for giving. He gave his life, his final gift, out of loyalty and love. Because of this sacrifice Karna traveled easily from this world to the next. His journey was blessed and watched over by Lord Krishna. Although Arjuna had won the battle, he knew that without Lord Krishna's help he could not have killed Karna. Indeed, Karna was truly the greatest archer in the whole wide world.

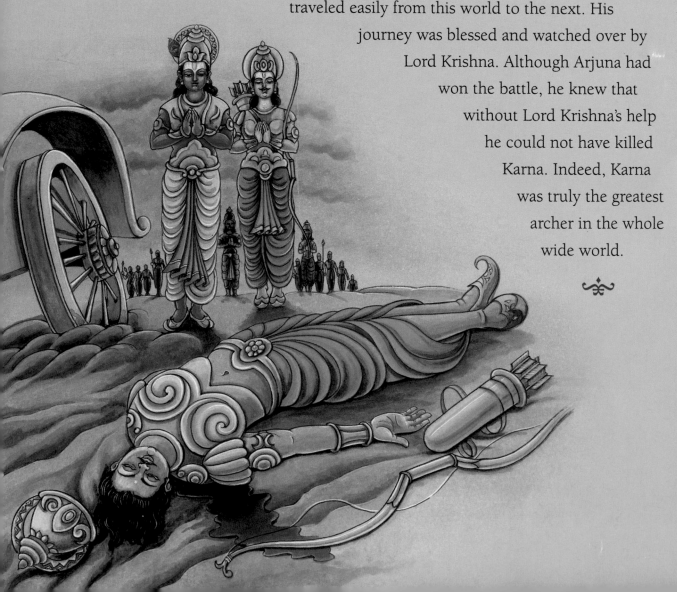

A Note to Parents and Teachers

The Mahabharata describes the inner struggles that people experience when they try to understand their real purpose in life. Though the epic's characters handle their struggles in different ways, Karna, abandoned at birth by his mother, finds himself at a disadvantage when it comes to understanding his place in the world. His is the story of many children who have been adopted—he loves his adoptive parents but knows nothing of his family of origin. Karna must always wonder where he came from and how he arrived at his childhood home. Nevertheless, his loving adoptive parents manage to provide him with a moral compass by the example of their own steadfast devotion to him. When he finally does learn about the circumstances of his birth, Karna's loyalty remains with the parents who took him in. Even when he learns that the Pandava princes are his own brothers, he keeps his promise to the wicked and greedy Duryodhana to honor the promise he made to a friend. By the moral code explained in the Mahabharata, this last act of loyalty is the only honorable choice for Karna. By giving his life, Karna allows the forces of good to prevail, while remaining true to his personal code of honor.

About the Illustrations

Sandeep Johari's illustrations were created with watercolor and tempera paints. Using transparent watercolors, the artist painted each picture in several steps. After outlining the figures, he filled them in, using three tones for each color to achieve a three-dimensional effect; next he applied the background colors. After each step he "fixed" the painting by rinsing it with water until only the paint absorbed by the paper remained.

Then the artist applied a "wash," using opaque tempera paints. After wetting the painting again, he applied the tempera to the surface until the whole painting appeared to be behind a colored fog. While the wash was still wet, he used a dry brush to remove it from the faces, hands, and feet of the figures. He let the wash dry completely, then rinsed the paper again to fix the colors. To achieve the desired color and emotional tone, each painting received several washes and fixes. Finally, the artist redefined the delicate line work of each piece, allowing the painting to reemerge from within the clouds of wash.

Please feel free to trace or photocopy this drawing of Karna for children to color.